THE BESIEGED

CHRISTOPHER W. MORIN

The Besieged

©2014 Christopher W. Morin

ISBN 13: 978-1-63381-023-5

Designed and produced by
Maine Authors Publishing
12 High Street, Thomaston, Maine 04861
www.maineauthorspublishing.com

Printed in the United States of America

To my 7th grade teacher, Mr. Stephen Cowperthwaite, who inspired and fueled my passion for both reading and writing short stories.

CONTENTS

Chapter 1

The Return Home

The frozen lake gradually came into view as a solitary figure atop snowshoes trudged along a trail cutting through a narrow mountain pass. The snow packed down hard with a crunch under each labored step the man took. It was deeper than normal, and even the sturdy wooden snowshoes couldn't prevent the man's feet and legs from sinking well beyond the depth he was accustomed to. This aggravated him as he was already very heavily laden with thick-layered fur coverings and a full pack of gear strapped to his aching back. As a further insult, the temperature was abominably cold.

Despite all the unwelcome barriers nature put in his way, the man plodded along until his destination was in sight. Just on the edge of the lake sat a small cabin. This was his home. He had built it with help just after his arrival to this new and extremely remote area of the world—a land called Alaska.

He had been an aspiring prospector. In 1897, upon hearing the news that gold had been found in the Klondike, he'd left his predictable and unfulfilling life in northern California for the promise of adventure in the hunt for gold and other treasures in the vast, largely unknown, untamed wilderness of Canada's Yukon. Like thousands of others drawn by the prospect of striking it rich, the man abruptly abandoned his old life, took everything he had of value, and invested it all in the opportunity to journey north into the unfamiliar reaches of Canada. He was thirty years old then.

Exceedingly unprepared for the adverse hardships that lay before him, the man struggled immensely, first on the sail up the coast to the Alaskan port of Dyea, then the trek overland on the Chilkoot Trail to the Yukon River, eventually leading to the town of Dawson near the Klondike gold fields in the late summer of 1898. Battered by constant fatigue, poverty, malnutrition, human deception, and the torturous cold, the man nearly gave up like so many thousands of others before him. However, his spirit was unbroken and he somehow prevailed. He staked his claim and searched endlessly for the elusive precious metal the entire world wanted—gold.

The prized element proved more intangible than the man had imagined. He panned for hours a day in the Klondike River finding little to nothing of value. He worked with others learning the art of gold prospecting, spending many nights encamped along the river's banks, hillsides, and creeks. When the search proved hopeless and supplies had dwindled to near nothing, the man and his party would make the trek back to Dawson to resupply and recover—never an easy task.

This scenario repeated time and again until weather or lack of able bodies made it impossible. The man, frustrated and at his wit's end, found himself spending more time dodging fists in the Dawson saloons or in his own wretched lodgings than at his claim searching for gold. He was constantly cold, hungry, broke, sick, and exhausted. He reached the breaking point in 1899 when the town of Dawson began to dry up and die. Unsanitary, unsafe, and suffering from serious supply shortages, the boomtown became totally unappealing to the penniless and desperate man.

One day in the summer of 1900 he simply gathered up all his meager possessions, abandoned his claim, and headed down the Yukon River to the Bering Sea where he planned to sail up to Nome, Alaska, to a new developing gold strike. It was both an ambitious and foolish quest for one hoping to rekindle the desire that had brought him in search of riches years earlier. He made it only as far as Tanana, deep in central Alaska, where he gave up entirely on finding gold and on life in general. He found a discarded, beat-up canoe on the banks of the Yukon and paddled many miles down a small, unnamed, and uncharted tributary that dumped into and ended at a medium-sized lake—also without a known name. It was here where the man built his home and decided to stay for the rest of his life, alone, nestled away in the Kuskokwim Mountains. That was twelve years ago.

Through all the adversity and hardships the man endured, the one that stood out the most, and also the one he'd been least prepared for, was the cold. He could not get over how indescribably cold it got in Canada's Yukon and in Alaska once winter had set in. It had nearly killed him on more than one occasion and was always a silent, lingering threat never to be ignored. Fire had saved his life and most certainly his limbs. If not for his swiftness in building a fire by himself or with the aid of others, he surely would have perished long before now. The man was never without sulfur matches and small scraps of dry birch bark. He kept both on his person at all times, even in fair weather.

Now it was January of the year 1913, and the man, now in his late forties, tramped up to the entrance of his cabin. Relieving himself of the burden of his heavy pack, weighted down with empty steel traps, he cursed while grabbing a shovel to clear away the snow built up against his door. The snow was deep and required much effort to relocate. He had been gone for only two days while tending his traps, but was very surprised at how quickly the freshly fallen snow had drifted and accumulated around his cottage. He shoveled long and deep, making sure to clear the doorway first, then all around the base of the walls. Next he cleared a path to his nearby meat shack, which wasn't stocked nearly as full of frozen fish and game as he would've preferred. It had been an unrewarding fall and brutally unforgiving winter.

After digging out his woodpile stacked next to the cabin, he entered his home with some frozen moose meat from the meat shack. It was to be his dinner that evening. The inside of the cabin was just as frigid as the outside air, and the man quickly realized he'd better build a fire fast before his bare hands and fingers went completely numb and lifeless—thus useless. He wondered just how cold it was. He had no thermometer but knew all the danger signs of deathly cold. Exposed hands, fingers, or feet that stung painfully before going completely numb in a matter of seconds was the first sign. A white cloud of moist breath that crackled and instantly froze to one's beard and face was the second sign. Inability to keep one's blood circulating to all vital parts of the body without constant thrashing and beating of the arms and legs was the third. The man was experiencing symptoms of all three. It had to be at least fifty below zero. He was sure of it. It was time to build a fire!

He crouched down in front of the fireplace and formed a nest of dried twigs and small tree branches. He placed a scrap of birch bark at the base and then ignited a match. The bark embraced the tiny flame quickly and it wasn't long before the remainder of the kindling was alight. The man nurtured the fragile fire until it was strong enough to take larger fuel. Steadily he fed it small twigs, graduating to larger sticks, ending eventually with full-size firewood. The fire grew with strength and soon a hearty blaze burned powerfully, providing much-needed warmth and light. The frostiness of the cabin gradually subsided, replaced by comforting, inviting heat that shielded life by keeping the harshness of the brutal cold at bay.

As the one-room cabin warmed, the man felt tingling sensations return to his hands and feet. He removed his heavy outer fur coverings and his fur hat. He was dressed in dark, baggy wool pants with brown suspenders and a dirty red plaid wool shirt. On his feet were thick wool socks and heavy moccasins. Around his waist was a gun belt supporting a leather holster that cradled a Colt single-action Army revolver. He removed the heavy belt and hung it on a wooden peg protruding from the wall.

He produced a metal spit with a sharpened end and rammed it through the frozen chunk of moose meat. He then laid it horizontally across two larger wide-based vertical rods with round notches cut in at the tips. The spit rotated in the notches with the help of a little crank the man attached last. When finished, he carefully slid the whole makeshift rotisserie over the fire to cook.

"Damn this cold," he said, realizing it was taking much longer to heat the small cottage than usual. He tugged at his black beard as he glanced out the small window that faced the lake to the rear. He could feel tiny drafts around the frame where the glass was not properly fitted to the wood. This made him angry and he feared the consequences if the glass were to break in such extreme cold. Window glass was a rare and precious luxury to have in such a remote area, and he had no replacement. In fact, supplies of all varieties were scarce. The man gazed around his small home and began to take inventory. His meat supply was dangerously low—a sad testament to the empty traps sitting in a heap outside his door. The trapping had been terrible of late and the hunting even worse. He had managed to shoot a small moose weeks earlier, but that was all there was—save for a few fish—hanging in his meat shack. He blamed the biting cold for keeping the animals hunkered down and difficult to lure to the traps.

Dry goods were running low too. His coffee sack was nearly empty, as was his sugar. He had a decent supply of salt on hand but not much use for it during this time of year when meat was easily preserved in the frigid Alaskan temperatures. He had a little flour in a canister but not nearly enough to make pancakes or biscuits. He had no eggs, bacon, butter, or powdered milk. Worst of all, he had no canned goods or jars of preserved foods like soups or vegetables. His small pantry was distressingly void of essential foodstuffs needed to last a long, hard winter. Even his precious whiskey and pipe-tobacco stores were in short supply.

The man's frustration with life's hardships and cruelty had made him excessively bitter and reclusive. His failures in gold prospecting had impoverished him, leaving him with limited options for bettering his situation. He became lost mentally, and stranded physically, in the vast wilderness that was Alaska. His dealings with people often left him feeling betrayed. He had been swindled more than once and had nearly lost his life over a crooked business deal gone sour. Over time he began to despise and distrust people in general. He dealt with them only when absolutely necessary and tried to avoid the ones overflowing with unbridled avarice. In time they became easy to spot.

The man had found his isolated corner of the world and had constructed his home with some help from two native tradesmen from Tanana. After hiring their services with lies and fabricated promises of payment in gold, he worked alongside them wondering how his debt would ultimately be settled. When the job was finished, the man showed little gratitude and even less compensation, which amounted to some furs, his sled, and the business end of his Winchester rifle. The tradesmen furiously made off with their meager pay and loudly swore their revenge. He never saw them again.

The cabin was made of logs cut from the forest that grew at the base of the mountains ringing the lake and river. The simple structure was small but sturdy. It had two four-pane windows, one in the rear that faced the lake and one in the front next to the door. The floors and roof were made from sawmill lumber and the fireplace and chimney were masonry brick. All the lumber, brick, and glass had been transported via boat down the river from Tanana, which was a painfully strenuous process, but one that paid off in the end. All the supplies that nature couldn't provide came from this one small town twenty miles upriver to the north. Besides that, there was only one other way out—through the narrow mountain pass to the west where the nearest native settlement of significance was over a hundred miles away.

The cabin was furnished with a table, two wooden chairs, a small bedframe underneath a thin feather-stuffed mattress with pillow, and a rocking chair that faced the fireplace. That was all. Next to the hearth was a small stack of wood and an iron poker. Cabinets above a small counter space held all the man's provisions—what little there were. He kept his clothes in an old trunk, while the rest of his gear and possessions were piled up in a corner or hanging from long pegs on the wall.

The man returned to the fireplace and rotated the moose meat so it would cook evenly. The room filled with the savory aroma of moose meat, making the man's mouth water. He was hungry, his empty stomach producing odd sounds. After several revolutions on the spit, the moose meat was finally cooked to the man's liking. He plated the meat and sat back in his rocking chair watching the fire as he ate. Occasionally he looked out the rear window. It had been cloudy and dark all day and now night was nearly upon him. He finished his small meal and gazed out at the frozen lake.

The air was unusually calm and frigid with no indication of any wind through the trees. The darkened skies were empty of winged life just as the landscape was barren of four-legged creatures. The peculiarities in the atmosphere coupled with the absence of wildlife were unmistakable signs pointing to one sure outcome—a storm. But what kind of storm? And how severe? These were the questions now swirling around in the man's head.

"That's just what I need," he muttered sarcastically while staring coldly out at the mountains. "Another Goddamned storm! As if everythin' weren't bad enough. I have a pack filled with empty traps, no money or gold in my pocket, hardly any supplies, and now Mother Nature to scrap with!"

He got up, spat into the fire, then uncorked his nearby whiskey bottle. He looked out the rear window again before taking a long draft. Just then it began to snow. The man shook his head in disgust.

"Why'd I ever come to this godforsaken land?" he grumbled bitterly. "Knowed nothin' but pain and misery these past fifteen years. What've I made of myself? What've I become? No fortune in gold...no easy livin'. Just nothin'...nothin' but hardship and struggle."

The man knew what he had to do and hated the thought of the difficult task before him. He needed supplies and he needed them badly. He'd have to get up early and make the trek up the frozen river to Tanana. His sled was long gone and so were the dogs he'd once owned to pull it. For several years now he'd relied solely on his own back and legs to transport the goods and materials he needed to survive through the cold season. The twenty-mile trip was never easy in wintertime. Even in normal conditions there was danger everywhere. Now, with the snow falling and the temperature being as low as it was, the odds of running into trouble grew exponentially. The thought did not sit well with him. Even more vexing was how he planned on paying for his supplies with no money.

"They'll extend my credit...they gotta. They won't let me go back with nothin'...not in this weather. It would be like condemnin' a man to death. They can't do that. They won't, neither. Can't let 'em."

With an angry attitude in defiance of the falling snow, the man threw open his door and rushed to the woodpile. His bare hands, fingers, and face rapidly numbed as he loaded up his arms with as many logs as he could carry. Stumbling back inside, he dropped the wood near the fire and crowded the dancing flames. He shivered hard for a moment until the absorbed heat cured his body of the shaking, stinging frostiness. He couldn't remember the last time he'd experienced such a vicious cold. Moreover, he was sure he'd never felt the effects of his body numbing so quickly in only a few seconds of exposure. No matter, he thought. He was safe in his warm cabin. He stoked the fire and watched it roar with delight, knowing it would protect him even if the temperature dropped to one hundred below. He rubbed his hands, snickered a little, then picked up his whiskey bottle before settling down in his rocking chair.

Chapter 2

The Monster in the Window

An hour passed and it was dark now. The only light came from the fire's glowing embers. The man had slipped off into a whiskey-induced half-drunken slumber. He was slouched back in his chair clutching the near-empty bottle. The wind and snow had picked up as the gathering storm drew closer. The man slowly opened his eyes as his ears alerted him to a peculiar noise coming from outside. Curiosity overcame his natural tendency to fall back asleep, so he rose up and staggered toward the back window.

The man looked outside into the darkness and saw nothing. He could hear the wind whooshing and quickly dismissed the odd sound as nothing more than that. He took a step toward his bed, longing for sleep, when suddenly the eerie sound returned. He listened close as his ears struggled to distinguish between the sound of the hissing wind and what seemed to be a long, drawn-out howl. With a bit of forced concentration spurred by an uneasy chill down his spine, the man was able to determine what he was hearing—a sound he had heard before, and dreaded.

"Wolves," he uttered. The man's thoughts immediately turned to the meat shack. He'd had problems in the past with wildlife raiding his food supply, and few things angered him more than being robbed by a critter. Wolves and bears were the biggest threat as the wooden shack was not very large or sturdy. Grizzlies had ripped through the walls with ease numerous times while wolves had dug around the rotten foundation like burrowing gophers to gain entry. The man cursed the day he'd decided against building a floor in the structure.

"Strange for wolves to be roamin' at night in such horrible weather," he said to himself. He hadn't seen a wolf in weeks and was in no hurry to confront one now. Nevertheless he knew he had to be on guard whether he liked it or not. His pitiful supply of hanging meat was all he had and he couldn't afford to lose it no matter how many supplies he was able to bring back from Tanana.

He tossed some birch bark and three logs onto the fire, bringing it back to full blaze. The concentrated scent of cooked moose meat lingered in the air, which he knew wasn't a good thing. He yearned to go back to his rocker, pretend he'd heard nothing, and fall away into a deep sleep. As appealing as that was, the man couldn't allow himself to do it. He sat on the edge of his bed watching the fire and listening intently to the sounds outside his walls. He went so far as to close his eyes so they didn't distract or interfere with the work of his ears. After a short time passed, he heard it again. Apart from the wind was the distinct sound of a howling wolf. Then he heard another—and then another!

Just then a scratching sound startled him. It was faint but unnerving. He turned to face the rear window. His eyes caught sight of a frighteningly dark silhouette, barely visible, seemingly reflecting off the glass in the firelight! The man leapt to his feet and backed away from the window. He grabbed for his kerosene lantern, fumbling with his matches before successfully lighting it. He thrust the brightness of the lantern at the window, revealing the terrifying sight of a wolf's upper torso! Standing on its hind legs, the animal peered inside with a fierce glare and bared teeth. Its front legs pressed against the frame while his claws slowly scratched and scraped down the glass.

The man recoiled in horror as his adrenaline-filled heart pounded madly at the sight of the brazen beast. The creature showed no fear and displayed signs of boldness unlike anything the man had ever witnessed in a wolf's behavior. He kept the animal in full view, never taking his eyes off it as he slowly backed away toward the wall where his holstered revolver was hanging. As the man retrieved his gun the wolf darted away out of sight amidst the noise of many distinct howls that seemed to surround the cabin.

Suddenly the man heard the sound of claws raking against cracking wood! He raced to get his socks and moccasins on before throwing open the front door and stepping out into the night. In one hand was his revolver while the other carried the kerosene lantern. The falling snow, caught up in the blowing wind, flew into his eyes while the glacial air hit him like a hammer, stopping him as if he had run into an invisible barrier of thick ice. Nevertheless, the man shined his lantern in the direction of the meat shack. He couldn't see much. The lantern wasn't powerful enough to cut through the stormy darkness and the shack was just too far away to see anything. However, it was no mystery what was happening. A pack of ravenous wolves was assaulting the rickety little structure, determined to devour every scrap of meat therein.

The man cocked his handgun and fired a shot into the air. He bellowed loud obscenities hoping to intimidate and scare off the predators. He lurched forward several steps until the shack was in range of his light. The wolves scattered in all directions but didn't leave. Instead they retreated into the darkness and encircled the man. Like shadowy ghosts, they slipped in and out of the light, affording the man only a short, uneasy glimpse of their movements. The man turned in sharp circles like a corkscrew with each growl he heard and every four-legged motion he saw. These animals were acting unnaturally aggressive and zeroing in on their next meal—a human victim! The man quickly realized he was surrounded and in imminent danger of being ripped apart and devoured by the vicious pack of hunters. As he thought this, his lungs and throat let out a fierce cry of anger followed by two more random bullet blasts from the revolver. He heard several animal footsteps scampering off into the distance. His last effort had managed to drive them away—for the moment at least.

Seemingly free of danger, the man hurried over to the meat shack. He shined his lantern and surveyed the damage. At first glance there didn't appear to be any serious problems until the man looked at the base of the door and saw what he was dreading. The bottom right side of the entrance had been rotting away for months and was the structure's Achilles heel. The wolves had apparently discovered this, and a cavity of broken wood large enough for one to squeeze through had been created.

As the man examined the hole, he felt his hands, feet, and face rapidly numbing. In fact, his whole body was beginning to shiver uncontrollably. In his haste to protect his meat stores from the wolves, he had not had time to put on his thick fur coverings, hat, or mittens.

The adrenaline from the confrontation was quickly wearing off and the man realized he would most assuredly lose the battle with the cold if he didn't get indoors instantly. He decided he would warm up inside first, then properly dress himself before returning to the meat shack with all his empty traps. He'd then deploy every one around the perimeter, creating an impenetrable defensive line bound to discourage or mortally ensnare any marauding wolf foolish enough to come back. If the whole pack returned, his Winchester rifle would sort them out.

Before returning to the safety of the cabin, the man looked down at the hole again and noticed a chunk of moose carcass barely protruding outward. He reached down and into the opening. As his right hand grasped the frozen hunk of meat he cried out in tormenting pain as a powerful set of jaws clamped down on his forearm! The man fell backwards and as he did, the jaws released him. Lying on his back in the snow with his right forearm badly bleeding, the man looked up as his attacker poked its head out of the hole and into the light of the lantern.

"Jesus Christ!" exclaimed the man as he locked eyes with the same wolf that had first appeared and terrorized him at his window. The beast growled and snarled, exposing its long, sharp fangs. The man saw the fur on its back stand up and he knew it was about to pounce! Desperately he groped for his fallen revolver only to come up with frigid handfuls of snow and ice. The man's hands were almost totally numb and without any sense of feeling. If he didn't find the gun in a matter of seconds his frozen fingers wouldn't be able to either grasp or fire the weapon.

The wolf squirmed its way out of the small hole in the door and leapt to the man's feet. It growled even louder and readied itself to leap onto the man's chest and plunge its teeth into his jugular! Just then the man's left hand passed over an irregular shape in the snow. He turned his head fast and saw his wrist resting on his gun. Unable to feel where the stock was, the man had to use his eyes to guide his fingers. With great effort he picked up the gun and pointed it at the wolf. His thumb, nearly dead with numbness, barely managed to pull back the hammer just as the beast sprang forward! With a flash and a mighty bang the wolf's chest imploded under the blunt force of the discharged Colt cartridge. The animal let out a whimper and its lifeless body crashed harmlessly to the ground.

The man got to his feet dazed and disoriented. He staggered a few steps in a circle before his mind began working clearly enough to force him to stop moving. Just then the pain of his wound hit him. He looked at his injured forearm covered in blood and snow and realized he had to get inside fast or risk bleeding to death, before he froze to death. He only looked once at the beast that had attacked him. Its black fur was already thinly coated white from the falling snow, and soon it would be entombed under several more inches–something the man did not want to see happen to himself. He briefly thought about trying to drag the carcass inside. He needed the meat and the animal's hide, but there was nothing he could do at the moment. He was too dazed, too cold, and far too weak.

With great struggle, the man cupped his frigid hands and managed to scoop up the lantern and revolver. He squeezed both hard to his chest and stumbled back to the cabin. Once inside he dropped his possessions on the table and rushed to the fire. His whole body shivered uncontrollably to the point where he felt his chattering teeth would shatter inside his mouth. He drew as close to the fire as he could. He tried to feed it more wood, but couldn't feel his fingers grasp the logs. His hands felt dead and he feared frostbite of the severity that would require amputation. The thought struck fear in his heart, triggering him to lie on his stomach and blow desperately on the red coals to produce hotter flames. Eventually the fire burned more impressively, giving him renewed hope.

He curled up on the floor in a tight ball. The snow and ice that had accumulated on his cheeks and beard gradually melted away, and he soon felt a stinging sensation return to his face. As his body's core warmed, the blood in his veins began to circulate more freely to his stricken limbs. With the aid of the fire, the man's hands and feet began to thaw. Soon they too began to sting and ache. The man happily welcomed the pain, as it was a sign of life in his precious extremities. Soon he was able to flex his fingers and wiggle his toes. As soon as his hands functioned again, he grabbed several logs and rejuvenated the fire until it was a roaring blaze.

With the fire taken care of, the man now focused his attention on the bloody mess that was his right forearm. The wolf's teeth had inflicted several puncture wounds that painfully oozed precious blood. It stained the floor and he began to feel faint. Looking around, he found an old torn shirt in his trunk that he wrapped around his arm tightly after dousing it in whiskey. It would have to do, for he had no bandages or other medical supplies. He fumbled around in one of his cabinets and found another bottle of whiskey; only this time he didn't apply it to his injured arm, but rather his parched lips and throat.

He collapsed in his rocker in front of the fire and drank heavily, hoping the liquor would ease the pain in his body and dull his mind. Soon his head was spinning to the point where he couldn't stand. His problems, severe as they were, slowly left his mind as his body began to shut down. He was exhausted, and sleep would overtake him very soon. Before he fell unconscious, one final plan formulated in his alcohol-clouded mind.

"Tomorrow...tomorrow I'll set those traps," he whispered. "Them wolves won't be back tonight. I showed 'em. They won't get my meat or me! I'll shoot every one of 'em dead, skin 'em, hang their dressed carcasses in my meat shack, and then sell their pelts in Tanana. Then I'll load up with all the supplies I need before coming home. Maybe even get someone to look at my arm. Yeah, that's what I'll do tomorrow...tomorrow."

The man dropped off into a deep sleep. Fire had saved him again and he was quite content to stay within the confines of its protection. As the blaze roared heartily, the wind outside blew stronger and the snow continued to fall at a rapid rate. As the man slept his mind was a dark and bitter void. He no longer dreamed of acquiring riches of gold and affluence or achieving high levels of prestige and power. He didn't dream of women or the joys of having a family. He no longer thought about exotic places or adventurous travel or even his past life back in California. Even the most pleasurable dreams of simple comfort and contentment never seemed to enter his head anymore. The thought of people crossed his mind least of all now. Still he slept soundly, filled with rancorous resentment toward life and those who had made it so unpleasant for him.

Chapter 3

Feeling Trapped

The man awoke in his rocker with a sore neck and a painfully inflamed forearm. He was very cold and could see his breath each time he exhaled. He looked at the cold, dark, and gray fireplace and then at the rear window, which let in the dull morning light. Neither sight provided him any comfort.

"Damn weather. Damn cold," he said while building a new foundation of twigs and sticks in the fireplace. "Stupid fool, I am," he added knowing how dangerous it was to let the fire go out in such extreme cold temperatures. "Gotta be more careful...might wake up dead," the man quipped after striking a match and placing it in the center of his kindling.

As the fire got going, the man noticed his wood supply was getting low. He'd have to bring a sufficient amount in from the woodpile before he left for Tanana. He grumbled at the idea of the additional labor but understood it was necessary. He looked out the rear window and was surprised the storm hadn't let up much. The skies were gray and the snow kept falling at a steady rate. Visibility was a little better as the wind had died down, but it would still be a long, hard trip. The man cursed at the thought of having to spend a night or two in town until the storm passed and it was safer to return home. Also he detested the thought of having to pay a doctor to treat his arm—provided he could find one. He knew he couldn't avoid the matter and he risked amputation if he tried to ignore it. Scary visions of his father, who had lost a leg assaulting Marye's Heights at Fredericksburg, ran through his mind. He couldn't afford to lose his arm and expect to survive...not in this wild and uncivilized part of the world.

The man strapped his revolver on his hip and then put on his furs, hat, and mittens. He decided he'd set his traps around the meat shack as originally planned, then strap on his empty pack and snowshoes to make the hard trek up the frozen river to Tanana. Knowing he'd have nothing to barter with, he began thinking of ways to whip up sympathy from the town's merchants so as to extend his tenuous line of credit. Maybe his wounded arm would draw some compassion and generosity? First things first, though, he had to bring in an ample supply of wood and some breakfast. He wondered if there was anything left or if the black wolf had gotten it all. He'd soon find out. There was a sense of urgency brewing inside him, as he didn't want to use up too much time. He could feel his arm slowly deteriorating with each throb and painful ache, while the weather wasn't improving either.

The man pushed open the door and instantly froze in place. Standing before him at a distance of about five feet was another wolf! Compared to the last one he had encountered up close, this one was bigger, looked much more ferocious, and was very much alive. The animal snarled at the man, exposing its teeth. Without thinking, he darted behind the door and pulled it shut just as the wolf sprang forward. It growled loudly and clawed at the door, showing tenacity the man had never seen previously. Wolves had raided his meat shack in the past, but they had never come close to the cabin or tried to force their way in. Normally, when in the presence of humans they acted like mischievous thieves rather than aggressive killers. Something was very wrong.

The man bolted the door, then went to the front window. To his astonishment, he saw several other wolves skulking around. He counted five at first, then seven. Finally he concluded there was a pack of eleven distinct predators just outside his walls. He wondered if they were the same animals that had been there last night. They were all exceptionally lean and very hungry-looking. Their eyes possessed wickedness and an aggression fueled by desperation. The man could see that this pack was starving and had reached the point of doing anything to survive—which meant going after human flesh!

The meat shack had been brought down. It was nothing but a pile of wood now. The wolves had torn it asunder while devouring the meager portions of meat within. To the man's further amazement, he saw the carcass of the wolf he'd shot dug out of the snow and ripped to pieces. The pack had cannibalized one of their own to satiate their deprivation.

"Just look at them nasty sons-of-bitches," the man said, observing the wolves that had all but surrounded the cabin. "Maybe them petty swindlers up in Tanana will be gettin' wolf pelts as payment today after all."

The man pulled his Winchester off its wall rack. It was a very accurate and reliable model 1873 lever-action rifle. He prized the gun as it paired nicely with his Colt single-action Army revolver. The .44-40 center-fire cartridge was interchangeable, allowing him to conveniently use the same load for both guns.

He worked the lever action forward. To his dismay, both the chamber and the magazine were vacant. He cranked on the lever several times to confirm his fear—the gun was empty. Without hesitation, the man went to the cabinet where he stored his ammunition. He reached for his cartridge box only to find it as barren as his rifle. He tossed the box down on the floor in frustration and started to search for any stray rounds that might be hidden out of sight. He checked his other cabinets, then his clothes trunk. He threw every article of clothing he had with a sewn-in pocket in a pile on the floor and searched them. He found nothing.

He went to the window and saw the wolves restlessly pacing. Some howled, while others growled and snarled. It was as if they were waiting for the precise opportunity to storm the cabin in force. He could see they were ravaged with hunger and undoubtedly very cold. It occurred to the man that the beasts were not just looking for a meal, but also some warmth and shelter. They could have all three if they could just get inside, and it looked as if they weren't going away anytime soon.

The man started to do some pacing of his own. He thought hard, trying to devise a solution to the problem at hand. He had to deal with the wolves first and above all else. Until they were dispersed the man was trapped. He couldn't leave the safety of the cabin to make the journey to Tanana. As soon as he opened the door he'd be preyed upon and dismembered. He had little to protect himself. His ax was buried in the snow by the woodpile and a hot fire poker would not fend off a whole wolf pack for very long. Neither would his knife. His traps were in his pack outside, carelessly neglected the night before. He thought of using fire, but realized he had nothing that would make a sufficient long-burning torch. Even so, there were just too many to face. There was the revolver, however.

The man drew his handgun and spun the cylinder. He removed the four spent cartridges and was somewhat relieved to see two good rounds left. But what good were just two bullets? At best he could bring down two wolves, but what about the other nine? Surely they would make quick work of him once his rifle went dry. He could yell at the top of his lungs and fire both shots into the air hoping to frighten off the hungry animals. That might buy him enough time to slip away and head up the frozen river toward civilization and more bullets. That was a big gamble, however. Even if he succeeded in scaring them off, they would most assuredly catch up with him once he was on his way. Defenseless, he would be ripped to pieces.

An hour passed. The man sat in his rocker, staring at the fire, waiting. There was little else that could be done. If he waited long enough, perhaps the wolves would tire and move on. Outside the snow was still falling at a steady rate and the frigid temperatures hadn't subsided. His injured arm throbbed with pain while blood began to drip through the saturated makeshift bandage. He wondered if the wolves could pick up the scent of his blood in the air. Perhaps that was why they were so stubborn about staying. The man looked at his arm and sighed. There was little he could do. It was infected and slowly festering. Even the alcohol wasn't helping. He wasn't sure of the severity of the wound. He just knew it hurt and needed to be properly treated soon or he risked losing it.

As the man watched the logs in the fire burn down, a frightening realization hit him. He slowly turned in the direction of the firewood supply. His head dropped, followed by another deep sigh upon remembering he was very low on wood and would need to bring more in soon or else lose his only source of heat and protection from the harsh weather. It was at this moment that the man fully understood the precarious situation he was in. He had practically no food, no adequate means of defending himself, a dwindling source of accessible wood, and an injured limb.

"My God, how'd I get into this mess?" the man whispered. "This is unnatural. The mischievous work of the Devil himself, I swear it is."

If the wolves didn't get him first, the cold would most assuredly kill him once the fire went out. Even if he could hold out deprived of fire, how long could he go without food? And even if he went hungry for days, how long would his strength last with his infected arm? Surely he'd catch a fever and that would do him in quickly without proper nourishment, warmth, and medicine to treat it.

Angry and irritated with his predicament, the man drew his revolver and pointed it upwards. He opened the side-loading gate, pressed the ejector rod, and let one of his two remaining rounds slide out into his hand. He holstered the handgun and retrieved his Winchester. Sitting back down in the rocker, rifle in hand, the man rhythmically tapped the bullet against the receiver just above the elliptical loading port. His mind went to work. He needed to find a solution—one that would remedy the situation with limited means at his disposal. Just then instinct took over. He pushed the bullet into the loading port and chambered the round with one quick action of the lever. For some reason he felt it best to have both guns loaded. The rifle was best suited for taking down a target at long distance, while the revolver was more useful in dealing with threats at close range.

The morning dragged on while the man impatiently observed his captors' movements through the front window. They patrolled and probed the cabin's perimeter looking for weaknesses that could prove opportune. He noticed they took interest in both windows, never venturing too far from either. Occasionally one would claw and try to dig at the base of the door hoping to tunnel its way in. At one point, the man was taken by surprise as he heard sounds coming from the roof! He surmised one of the wily creatures had jumped up onto his woodpile, then onto the rooftop.

The sound of movement coming from above was unsettling and aggravating. The snow-laden roof was pitched but not enough to discourage an audacious wolf from digging in and making itself comfortable next to the warm brick chimney. The thought angered the man to the point that he wanted to put a shot through the roof where he thought the animal was. He quickly and wisely dispelled the foolish notion.

Morning soon turned into afternoon. The man clicked open his pocket watch. Upon seeing the time, he cursed loudly. He couldn't make it to Tanana today even if he *was* able to leave. It was too late, the weather was too unforgiving, and the journey too treacherous without ample daylight hours. The man conceded that the day was lost and he could do nothing but continue to wait and hope the wolves would move on during the night. Certainly the sharp cold would drive them away. Even their natural thick coats of fur couldn't protect them against such harsh temperatures indefinitely.

As the hours passed and darkness set in, the man scrounged around looking for anything edible he may have forgotten he had stored away. He found nothing. He brewed up the last of his coffee over the fire. As he sat back in his rocker sipping the hot beverage, to which he'd added some sugar, he heard the wolves begin to bay again in unison. He listened closely. This particular howl sounded more like a collective warning rather than a natural communicative sound amongst animals. The man took heed and began to wonder if he had just been issued a death sentence.

Once in bed he found it hard to sleep. The temperature inside began to drop as the fire burned with less intensity. He had begun rationing his wood hours earlier and was now beginning to feel the effects. With a great sigh he estimated he could keep the fire burning softly until sunrise and would have just enough wood to last a good part of the next day, provided he allocated it wisely. He knew he had to keep sufficient wood burning during the night, or risk freezing. He could tell, even without a thermometer, that the temperature outside had dropped substantially again. He wondered if it had reached seventy below yet.

Heavily bundled in his bed between thick wool blankets and his furs, the man tried desperately to sleep. His arm ached severely and began to give off a very worrisome and pungent odor. The man felt sweat beads begin to form on his forehead; he was shivering and could feel his body developing chills associated with a fever. He was experiencing the early signs of sickness, and that was more life-threatening than a hundred hungry wolves, especially if left unchecked. He tried to put it out of his mind. Sleep was the first priority now.

The man tossed and turned on his thin mattress but couldn't get comfortable. He was cold, hungry, and in pain. He rolled to his side and watched the tiny flickering flames escape up the chimney. He wanted to get up and nourish the fire so that it burned with ferocity strong enough to combat the harsh temperatures assaulting his home; however, he knew he couldn't and had to smother the temptation. Resisting the urge, the man rolled over on his back and shut his eyes tightly in hopes he would fall asleep soon.

The cabin was eerily dark. The man could hear the wind blowing heavily outside and could feel the sheer weight of the storm as it bore down upon him. He couldn't help but continually wonder if the detrimental weather would eventually overwhelm the wolves, forcing them to succumb or move on, seeking more adequate shelter. Their resolve had been uncanny and it was becoming disturbingly clear that their persistent doggedness for meat would defy the weather and anything else that stood in their path. He tried to put the menacing brutes out of his mind as well as the hard-driving storm and his painfully afflicted arm. He attempted to reassure himself that all would be better in the morning and that he just needed to fall asleep. Sleep was the best escape from all that ailed the bitter, reclusive man, and he summoned it as often as he could.

Try as he might, the man couldn't drift off into a deep slumber. Occasionally he'd doze only to be awakened by the sound of the storm's whipping winds, the unpleasant sensation of cold air creeping in through the cracks in the walls, or a painful twinge in his arm. After feeling a stream of cold air run over his face, the man went against his best judgment, got up, and tossed another log on the ever-shrinking fire. As the flame recouped a small measure of strength, the man huddled down close to its fiery core. He watched the flames lap against the sides of the freshly added log and closely guarded the cherished warmth and light it provided. He found a moment of solace under the protection of the fire as his chilled bones absorbed the welcome heat. A few minutes passed and the man got back into bed with renewed confidence for a peaceful rest.

Suddenly, the man's comfort was brusquely shattered. A strange noise seized his eardrums, causing his gut to tingle in fear and his eyes to open wide. Above the sound of the storm was an unholy yowl from all eleven wolves! With a jolt, the man sought cover beneath his blankets much like a child trying to hide from an imaginary monster. He was accustomed to the sounds of Alaskan wildlife and certainly was no stranger to the distinct growls and howls of wolves; however, this unusual baying had a sinister tone, like shrieking ghosts hovering all around him!

Rattled, he got up and reached for the lantern. Just as he did he hesitated, stopping dead in the center of the room. He looked to the door upon hearing the resumed sounds of claws scratching and digging against the wood at the base with renewed intensity. His head then whipped upward after hearing several sounds indicating movement on the roof. Lastly he cringed upon realizing the wolves were at both windows. He could hear their claws raking against the glass and was terrified of what would happen if they managed to break through the thin, fragile barrier that was keeping them out as well as the deathly cold. The man scrambled for his matches, then the light resting on the table.

"What kind of demons possess these confounded creatures?" he asked with uneasy annoyance as a fresh and lively glow pushed aside the darkness with the reigniting of the lantern. Light, like the burning fire, was his ally—this he knew—and he'd use it to his every advantage, even as a potential weapon.

With the room lit up the man was more at ease. He made the lantern as bright as possible and held it up close to the front window. The light acted as a deterrent, forcing the wolves to back away as they didn't like the beams shining directly in their eyes. The man repeated the same action at the rear window. When satisfied he had discouraged the wolves enough to stay away from the glass, he set the lantern down on the table, dimming it as he angrily noticed it was running low on kerosene.

"Is there anythin' I have in *abundance*?" he asked loudly and sarcastically, knowing full well what the ill-fated answer was. "Yes there is," he said, adding, "I got plenty of pain and misfortune! If them two qualities were gold, I'd be the richest man in the world!"

The man sighed and gently rubbed his aching arm. The swelling was noticeably worse and his throbbing head continued to perspire. His throat was dry and scratchy and his mind dull from the developing sickness and lack of sleep. He was also starting to feel weak from food deprivation. The man reached for the only substitute for medicine he had—whiskey.

"If this don't help, nothin' will," he said before guzzling down the few remaining swallows. After he was satisfied he had drained it of every drop, he discarded the empty bottle and crawled back into bed with his Colt in easy reach. Just as he had hoped, it wasn't long before the effects of the alcohol, combined with his already weakened state, brought on sleep. There was imminent danger all around him and exceedingly limited measures of defense at his disposal; however, the need for sleep was absolute. He'd never make it out without a long rest, especially in his already declining state of health. Fortune, for once, was on his side as he was able to slumber, blissfully oblivious to the threats all around him.

Chapter 4

The Planned Trek

A cold chill swept over the man's face as he slowly opened his eyes. He had slept several hours undisturbed. It was freezing and still relatively dark in the cabin, yet he knew it was very early in the morning. He immediately looked to the fire, which to his dismay had totally burned out along with the lantern he had foolishly left lit and un-attended. His bleary eyes then looked around the cabin to see if anything appeared out of the ordinary. Nothing struck him as odd. He heard no sound from the wolves.

He sat up, coughing loudly while keeping his blankets tightly wrapped around him. He had the chills and was very feverish. His arm neither looked nor felt any better. It was badly infected and he knew he needed treatment without any further delay. He stood up and could see it was still snowing outside. Upon first glance out the rear window, he discovered it was difficult to distinguish between the natural features of the land, lake, and forest as everything was covered in a thick, white, uniform blanket of snow. He cursed at the sight of it.

"Damn! Gonna be hard travelin' in this mess. Gotta get going soon or won't be no chance of gettin' up to Tanana. Weather'll sock me in fast. Won't be able to go nowhere for days if I don't get moving. Won't make it back, that's for certain, but what's a night or two in Tanana? Worth it if it saves my arm. Just hope the doc's around."

The man started to move with a sense of urgency. He had to build another fire—there was no getting around that. He hurriedly stacked up the little kindling he had left, and with trembling, cold hands set it ablaze with one strike of a sulfur match held against a scrap of birch bark. As the fire grew in strength, the man fed it liberally with his limited wood supply, feeling confident the weather had driven away the wolves and that he'd be able to bring in all he would need from the woodpile outside.

The cabin warmed and the man wasted no time getting ready. He looked at his pocket watch and estimated he had just enough time to make it to Tanana before dark. He coughed repeatedly and cursed the sickness flowing in his veins. He put on extra socks and laced up his moccasins very tightly. He stood by the fire for several minutes warming his clothes and trying to absorb every ounce of heat his ailing body would allow. He yearned to stay by the blaze and relish its protective, life-giving warmth, but he knew he couldn't. He had to abandon it and bravely strike out into the cold or else face certain death in a matter of a few short days.

The man strapped on his revolver, then his hat, mittens, and thick fur coverings. He propped up his Winchester next to the door. He'd grab that last after he uncovered his pack and snowshoes, which were undoubtedly buried under several inches of snow. Then, after lugging in some firewood and putting some in his pack to take with him, he'd be off on his treacherous journey upriver. That was his plan. There wasn't a man alive who wouldn't have called him a fool for setting out in such abominable conditions, but he had no choice. He would surely die otherwise.

The man unbolted the door and pushed on it, fully expecting it to open with relative ease. To his surprise, the door barely moved. The man pushed harder to no avail. It felt as if a mighty force was pushing back on the other side, keeping him pinned indoors. He knew exactly what it was. Enough snow had fallen over the past two nights to effectively block the base of the outwardly opening door.

With an immense heave, the man forced open the door about five inches. Like a prisoner trying to tunnel his way out of a jail cell, he dug away at the exposed snow with his good arm until enough was cleared to open the door a bit farther. He dug longer and harder until he was able to squeeze his whole skinny body out. The man sucked in his gut and climbed outside into the snow. He grabbed his nearly buried shovel and started clearing away the snow around the door, hoping to find his snowshoes and pack. He was pleased the wind had died down considerably and hoped the snow would stop altogether. What had fallen was unusually deep but not totally impassable with the aid of snowshoes. The trip would be longer, harder, and more dangerous than usual, but he was out of options. He'd have to risk it. After toiling with the shovel for several minutes, he again noticed the bitter chill in the air. It wasn't the buildup of snow along the route, the threat of wild animals, or even his injured arm that worried him the most—it was the cold. That alone could kill a man faster than numerous other dangers combined. The man feared the cold and knew he had to be prepared to face it.

As he continued to dig out his gear by the door, he warily looked around. All seemed quiet and still aside from the falling snow and occasional frigid gust of wind. Then suddenly something caught his attention. He noticed a well-rounded mound of snow about twenty feet directly in front of him. The shape seemed peculiar and the harder he looked at it the more he thought it had moved! He knew he was feverish and his mind wasn't as sharp as it should be, but he couldn't help but wonder if what he was seeing was real or an illusion caused by the combination of his sickness and Mother Nature playing a prank on him. Whatever the case was, the man was intrigued enough to reach inside his door and grab the Winchester. With rifle in hand, he took two steps forward, sank knee-deep into the snow and tried to get a better look at the mysterious mound playing tricks with his mind. A minute passed by as the man stared intently, keeping his eyes locked on the same position. Then without warning, the mound of snow shifted from beneath!

"Goddamn, it ain't my eyes...somethin's under there," he said, raising the rifle and training the barrel on the center of the rounded snow heap in front of him. Just then he heard a noise from behind as a sizable portion of snow and ice cascaded down upon his neck and back.

Caught by surprise, the man spun around. He looked up toward the roof in terror as a large gray wolf leapt off the edge and pounced on top of him! He was knocked to the ground as the Winchester flew out of his hands. He shouted in fear, trying desperately to fend off the wild animal's sharp, stabbing teeth and razorlike claws. He kicked his legs and flailed his arms, hoping to break free of the wolf's hold on him. The vicious animal clawed at the man's face and upper torso, ripping through his furs and shirt in many places. The man cried out in pain before managing to get both hands around the beast's neck, preventing it from sinking its jaws into his jugular vein.

"You goddamned four-legged bastard from hell," he shouted, rolling over on top of the animal. "I'm gonna throttle you good then skin your mangy hide before you can suck your last breath!"

The wolf snarled with ferocity and aggressively clawed at the man's throat. He yelled out in pain, and with a great surge of adrenaline, picked the beast up with both hands and flung it as far as his tired muscles could manage. With a yelp, the wolf tumbled a few feet away. Unfazed, the animal scrambled to its feet, and with a vicious fang-baring growl, primed itself to lurch forward for another strike at the man's throat.

Quickly, he scrambled to his feet and could see the impression his dropped rifle had made in the fallen snow. He reached down for the Winchester, managing to pull it out of elbow-deep snow. Bringing the rifle to bear, the man fumbled with the lever, hammer, and trigger, swiftly realizing he couldn't properly grip or discharge the gun with his thick mittens on. The man wrenched off both hand coverings, but not before the wolf had sprung up at him. Unable to get off his sole remaining shot in time, the man speedily flipped the gun on end, grabbed it by the barrel, and wielded it like a club. The butt caught the wolf's skull in midair and cracked it open, sending the predator down to the ground with a drawn-out whine. Unsympathetic, the man drew his sheath knife and slit the animal's throat where it lay.

"You won't be troublin' me no more, you wretched spawn of the Devil. Let your entire infernal pack come back here to threaten and steal from me again. I'll line 'em all up beside you...one by one with my bare hands if necessary!"

Just as the man finished cursing out the fresh kill, his eyes were again drawn to the mysterious heap of snow. This time he knew his mind wasn't playing tricks on him as the undulating white mass moved and rolled until what was underneath was chillingly revealed. The man's eyes opened wide and he looked toward the heavens in both fear and disgust as if to infer that the Almighty was playfully toying with him to make good on his last statement.

The man lowered his eyes to confront what lay in front of him. Climbing out of the snow were several threatening single-mindedly hungry wolves. They unfolded themselves from a tight balled-up accumulation and began to fan out dangerously after shaking the snow off their furry backs. The man now realized that the pack had never left at all. The weather hadn't driven them off. They had simply huddled together, forming one large, warm, protective mass of fur to pass the night and wait for the right opportunity to attack. It was a successful ambush and the man wondered how he'd been so easily and foolishly drawn into their trap.

As the angry animals slowly began to move in, the man thought of making a dash for the door and retreating inside to the safety of the cabin. Then he hesitated. What good would it do? Again he'd be trapped as the wolves laid siege to his unsustainable home. These predators weren't going anywhere and he'd surely perish imprisoned in his cabin. He had to make a stand. He had to get to Tanana. He had to fight now or lose everything.

The man counted ten wolves. They formed a semicircle, trapping and pinning him against the front of the cabin. As the ferocious creatures growled, snarled, and yipped, slowly inching their way forward in unison, the man's clouded and exhausted mind went to work. With a quick surge of adrenaline, he grabbed the dead wolf's body by the legs and spun it around in a momentum-building circle. At the right moment he let go of the carcass, hurling it at the feet of the wolves flanking him on his left. The four wolves nearest the body immediately pounced on it in a violent feeding frenzy. The distraction bought the man enough time to grab the Winchester. With his exposed hands starting to go numb, he worked the lever forward and back, cocking the hammer, readying it to drop on the chambered round. With quick aim, he sighted the nearest threat and squeezed the trigger. The bullet exploded out of the barrel and slammed into the side of its intended target. The wolf was killed instantly while the others around it instinctively backed away, jolted by the discharged rifle.

The man mechanically worked the gun's lever action to eject the spent round, knowing a fresh one wouldn't be replacing it. However, as he hoped, two others in the pack preyed upon the newly slain animal, now hungrily tearing at its warm, bloody flesh. The man turned his attention to the last two predators who were ignoring the others and focusing squarely on him.

He dropped the Winchester and reached for his revolver; however, before he could pull it free from the holster, the wolves lunged, knocking him off his feet! They bit and clawed at him trying desperately to clamp their jaws around a vital artery in the leg or neck. The man shouted out in anger and fear, thrashing his arms and legs with all the remaining strength left in his body. As he flailed, he felt his right hand drag across his knife, which he had unknowingly dropped earlier. His fingers clutched the handle, immediately driving it upwards into the belly of the wolf that was going for his throat. But before the blade silenced the struck animal for good, its jaws bit into the man's right shoulder, causing him to cry out in excruciating pain. He twisted the knife and jerked it free while pushing the dead animal off him. Then, without thought, he plunged the knife into the neck of the second attacker biting and clawing at his legs. The animal yelped and jerked away so hard that the blade ripped free of the handle. The stricken predator fell to the ground and slowly expired, its blood staining the white snow red.

Powered solely by adrenaline and the instinct to survive, the man, badly hurt, pulled himself to his feet and drew his revolver. Without the ability to think clearly, he cocked the hammer and fired out of sheer rage. His last remaining bullet smashed into the skull of another able wolf, knocking it off its feet, killing it instantly. Drawing his remaining breath, the man yelled at the top of his lungs, hoping his voice—his last weapon—would strike enough fear into the hearts of his attackers and successfully drive them off. He was partially right.

The man's voice did spook the animals, but it wasn't fear that drove them away; it was the fact that there was now enough fresh meat to feast on to fill their empty bellies. The man grew dizzy and sick to his stomach. He began to wobble. The last sight he saw was the remaining wolves dragging off the carcasses of their dead to devour in peace and shelter from the weather. They disappeared into the woods, but not before bellowing out a haunting howl—a reminder of their strength, or perhaps a warning. It was the last thing he could remember.

≈⌒⌐ Chapter 5 ⌐⌒≈

Pain and Suffering

The man woke up shivering, feeling numb in some areas, great pain in others. He didn't know where he was at first or how he'd gotten there. Strangely enough, he thought he was dead, but didn't believe a dead man could feel such pain. Soon his senses functioned well enough that he could tell where he was and begin to piece together what had happened—and more importantly, what to do next.

He was facedown on the cabin floor. The door was open a few inches and a considerable amount of snow had blown in and piled up. The man could barely feel his frozen hands and his sore, stinging feet were not much better off. Despite his pain and numb appendages, with great effort he managed to push himself off the floor and slowly get to his feet. Once upright, he tried stomping his feet to regain circulation and feeling. Though very weak, the effort paid off as the stinging increased, reassuring him that blood flow had been somewhat restored. Next were the hands. He thrashed his arms and hands, coated in frozen blood, against his body hoping to revive any sensation. He thumped and beat them until he was dizzy and had to stop for fear of passing out again. He knew he had to act fast, as the cold once again threatened to take his limbs if not his life.

Unable to feel his fingers, the man cupped his hands and was able to use them like pincers to seize the door handle and pull the door completely shut, thus cutting off the icy cold stream of air flooding the cabin. Next he collapsed inches from the fireplace, his face near the ash bed scanning for any faint sign of lingering combustion. He drew a breath and slowly blew away the cold, gray top layers of ash hoping to reveal some tiny glowing red embers beneath. At first there was nothing. Then a tiny speck of red emerged from the seemingly endless mass of gray. The man blew a little harder until enough leaden ash was dislodged to reveal even more glowing coals not quite burned out.

The man praised his luck as he now knew all was not lost. Using his eyes to guide him, he reached into his small kindling pile of teeny twigs and birch bark. Unable to feel anything, he again visually guided his hands like pincers and scooped up enough to deposit on the minuscule bed of embers. Some of the more fragile sparks immediately burned out under the smothering weight of the kindling, but enough remained aglow for the man to go to work. He again got close to the bed of ashes and began to blow. With each controlled gasp he tried to breathe new life into the dying embers. As they brightened with every labored breath, the man prayed a tiny twig, scrap of dried grass, or fragment of precious birch bark would start to smolder.

He blew and blew, watching the prized embers burn out one by one. Panic started to set in, as he knew he'd never successfully be able to ignite, let alone retrieve, a match from his pocket with his dead fingers. He continued to puff away until only one small cluster of red cinders remained. With hopes fading fast, the man stopped channeling his exhausted breath onto the ashes. As he did this, he noticed a hairline wisp of smoke start to rise from a shred of charring birch bark. Gradually the smoke grew as the bark smoldered. Within seconds a tiny flame sparked to life! He knew he had to work fast. He clumsily poked and prodded with his dead fingers, gently trying to move other pieces of kindling near the smoldering birch bark. To his dismay, he nearly smothered the tiny core of the flame with one blundering motion of his useless hands. However, as if luck were on his side, a small patch of dried grass fell onto the flame, causing it to flourish with strength.

"Yes, yes...that's it," the man said as the little solitary flare slowly began to build and spread out onto the adjacent pieces of kindling. "Thank God," he whispered while reaching for more scraps of birch to nourish the fragile newborn fire.

Soon the flames grew big enough to take larger twigs, then small sticks of wood. The man held his hands close to the fire desperately hoping some form of sensation would return to his fingers. In the meantime he continued to use his hands and arms as pincers to move small sticks from the kindling pile onto the developing blaze. He kept at it until the pile was nearly gone and the fire was strong enough to burn on its own without further tending.

The uncontrollable shivering eventually subsided as the man steadily warmed. Holding his hands and feet in front of the hottest-burning area of the fire, he silently willed his limbs to come back to life. First, the stinging in his feet grew in strength then gently ebbed away. He could feel his toes wiggle inside the wool socks and moccasins. After a few minutes passed, he knew they'd be all right. With that he turned his full attention to his cut, frozen, blood-soaked hands.

Try as he might, the man couldn't make his fingers move. He thrashed his hands against the sides of his legs hoping to jar them back to some semblance of operable condition; however, that plan of action proved ineffectual and tiresome. With his little remaining strength waning fast, he was forced to rely solely on the heat of the fire to inject life back into his paralyzed limbs. He hoped it wasn't too late. He feared the surgeon's disfiguring saw more than death itself.

The fire burned progressively and the man started to lose hope. He surmised that beneath the dry bloody mess, his hands were badly frostbitten and would need to be amputated. As his anxiety grew he became increasingly desperate. He beat his hands hard against his legs one last time hoping to feel something...anything...and then without warning it happened—pain. Glorious and wonderful pain slowly began to creep down into his fingertips. The lines from his brain to his hands hadn't been totally cut! The man rejoiced with a feeble smile as he continued to hold his hands up to the fire's warmth.

Little by little the soreness in his knuckles increased. The rough feeling of pain was accompanied by a pleasant warming sensation. Underneath the intense smarting and discomfort resided a blossoming layer of warmth the man could sense pulsing through his fingers. Just then he saw his thumbs twitch ever so slightly. He concentrated hard and within a few minutes all his fingers were moving, but barely and with considerable pain and effort. His joints were swollen and locked up like seized machinery run heavily without lubricating oil. He'd have to endure it, for the alternative was far less appealing.

He painfully rose to his feet and slowly stripped off his tattered outer coverings and hat. It was then that he realized just how injured he was. His hands, arms, neck, and chest all had sustained lacerations from the wolves' claws and teeth. Some of the cuts were superficial and would heal easily in time, while others were more serious, requiring immediate attention. His fingers fumbled with the buttons on his shirt and the suspenders over his shoulders, but with a little extra effort, he soon had both off and was examining his bare upper torso. He looked at the bite marks on his shoulder and concluded they weren't as painful or as deep as his original arm wound. Nevertheless, they hurt and were just as prone to infection. He looked at the bloody shirt wrapped around his throbbing, swollen forearm and knew he had to do something. He was in pain and losing blood.

He looked to his wall where his metal washtub was hanging on a peg. He used the large basin primarily for laundering clothes and occasionally himself when he saw fit and actually had soap to do it with. He took it down and began scooping the heap of melting snow beside the door into it. Once all the snow was transferred, he pulled the tub close to the fire and watched it melt. Using a wooden dipper, he ladled out some to drink, hoping to ease the pain in his parched and sore throat. He then waited for the water to warm.

After feeding the fire with his last remaining big log, the man removed the rest of his clothing and stepped into the tub. He sat down in the lukewarm water. The basin was just big enough for him to sit with legs crossed. He splashed clean water onto his face and upper body, washing away the blood and turning the tepid, clear water a bright red. Gently and painfully he cleansed his angry wounds with a bar of Ivory soap and some salt he'd added into the bathwater. Though certainly not a doctor, the man had knowledge of bacteria and the sickness it caused. He didn't know if the salt helped, but he theorized that if salt could preserve fish and game long after butchering, then maybe it could preserve his own wounded flesh—at least long enough for him to get to real medical help. He paid extra attention to his wounded arm.

"God, don't it hurt," the man said as he slid the salty, wet bar of soap across his cuts. "Gonna need to get me some extra medicine and bandages up in Tanana. Need to have 'em on hand around here from now on. Them crooks in town gotta extend my credit. They can't deny that to a tore-up man leakin' blood like a sieve. Damn 'em if they even try."

After soaking a good while the man got out of the tub and dried himself by the fire. He then went to his trunk and tore strips of cloth from old shirts to use as bandages. He secured the cloth tight around his bitten shoulder and arm—the most serious wounds. He dressed himself in a fresh flannel shirt and wool pants that weren't shredded and blood-soaked. Once clothed, he scooped a dipper of water from a small barrel and poured some sugar into it before drinking it down. He knew the sweet potion would do little for his growing sickness, but he hoped it might help suppress his enormous hunger. With his meat supply gone, there was simply nothing left to eat.

Hungry, hurt, sick, and exhausted the man sank down into his rocker and concentrated on staying warm by the fire. It was very late in the day and he knew he couldn't go anywhere. He turned his head and looked out the rear window. To his dismay, it was still snowing. That sight, coupled with all his other problems, caused his spirits to sink and his clouded mind to succumb to fatigue. His eyes shut and his head dipped. He knew tomorrow would be a monumental challenge and test to his very survival. He didn't need whiskey to fall asleep this time, which was good, for he didn't have a single drop left anyway.

"At least I got a few of them damn bastards," he said, adding, "They won't be botherin' me again. Tanana...tomorrow...Tanana." With that, he fell unconscious.

Chapter 6

Unrelenting

The wind gusted and fresh snow fell at a greater rate as a new and more powerful storm collided with the remnants of the old, crashing into the region during the night. The unresponsive man, slumped to the side in his rocker, stricken with full-blown fever, was spent and oblivious to the formidable weather encompassing his home. Even the vigorously chilled air, seeping through the cracks in the walls, overpowering the heat produced by the diminishing fire, couldn't rouse the man to consciousness.

Time passed. The weather raged on and night turned into day. The man hacked out a series of loud coughs that brought him back from his state of heavy sleep. He leaned forward in the rocker and rubbed his aching, sweaty brow. His throat was sore and he continued to cough intermittently. He was weak and his legs nearly buckled underneath him as he went for a dipper of water. He cursed at his sickness, knowing full well the danger of fever.

The fire needed attention as the temperature inside was uncomfortably cold. No flames were visible but there was still a solid foundation of warm coals upon which to construct a new blaze. The man weakly turned to his stacked wood supply only to stop and stare at the worrisome sight. Remembering that he had been unsuccessful in replenishing his indoor supply because of the wolf situation, the man somberly looked down at the five remaining sticks of wood flanked by a smattering of unimpressive kindling scraps.

"It'll have to do for now," he said after tossing two pieces on the coals. Within minutes the logs caught fire and began to burn steadily. Just then the man noticed how unusually dark it was in the cabin. He reached for his pocket watch and saw that it was nearly noon!

"My God, how long has it been?"

The man's mind was unclear and he knew he wasn't thinking straight because of the fever, but he estimated he had been unconscious for nearly sixteen hours! He cursed loudly upon realizing it was too late to start out for Tanana. He'd never make it in the dark and would end up losing his way or perishing in the cold. He went to the front window and looked out in horror at the leaden skies pouring down a furious onslaught of heavy windswept snow. It had accumulated so quickly that it was now creeping past the base of the glass of both windows. The man had seen heavy snowfall before, but nothing like this. This was shaping up to be the worst storm he had ever seen. The landscape all around was nothing more than an unrecognizable mass of white. Even the mountains were obscured by the unrelenting snowfall.

With the journey to Tanana decidedly out of the question yet again, the man hurriedly dressed in his outer coverings in an attempt to venture outside, clear a path to his buried woodpile, and retrieve a supply of much-needed firewood and hopefully some of his gear, such as his mittens, his traps, the knife blade, and the Winchester, all now lost under a deep and heavy blanket of snow. The man unlatched the door and pushed hard on the handle. It did not budge. He pushed harder but couldn't open it an inch. He banged and pounded with his fists to no avail. Next he raised his legs and tried to kick open the stubborn door like a mule, succeeding only in aggravating his wounds and tiring his already weakened body. Returning to the front window, the man peered outside and could see the door was blocked by snow nearly chest high! Unsure of what to do next, he stumbled over to his bed and crumpled on the mattress. He closed his eyes to try to ease the dizziness in his head. His strength was waning as the sickness coursing through his body deepened.

"What I done to deserve this? Am I truly cursed? It ain't my time... not yet. I've sinned, but I won't die like this. You can test me, almighty God, but I won't break...not before a hungry wolf pack, not before the scoundrels in Tanana, not before this devilish weather, and not before you! I'll survive this! Damn all who get in my way! I ain't gonna die a prisoner in my own home!"

No sooner had he uttered the defiant words than a sharp pain shot through his arm. He tried to ignore it, dreading even to look at the wound for fear of what he might discover. His shoulder was not much better off and the other assorted claw marks, etched all over his upper body, were itchy, inflamed, and often bled when he was forced to scratch them. He needed medical care; moreover, he needed a way to get to it. His situation was becoming utterly untenable.

There was nothing that could be done as long as the storm raged on overhead. The man acknowledged this and accepted the fact that he was immobile until the skies cleared. He decided he would wait out the weather and then take his chances making the trek to Tanana. With the door blocked, he envisioned breaking a window and climbing out onto the snow. He'd then dig with his hands for all he was worth until he found his shovel and the rest of his gear—most importantly, his snowshoes.

"But I got no mittens," he remembered. "Them's buried somewhere outside."

He knew he couldn't dig for long with bare hands. They'd freeze and his fingers would grow numb until they broke off like brittle icicles.

"I'll just have to wrap 'em tight with shreds of old clothing like I done when making the bandages," he said, turning his head toward the clothes trunk.

He lay still, keeping his eyes closed. Trying to ignore the fever-induced symptoms clogging his mind, he turned his full concentration toward the next immediate problem.

"Wood won't last much longer," he uttered. "Can't get to the pile outside. Won't be long before she burns out. Them three sticks won't last through the night. Have to bundle up best I can and take the cold...just take it."

The man opened his eyes and turned his head toward the prancing flames of the fire. It burned with vigor, yet its power and warmth would diminish quickly as the lack of fuel, coupled with the cabin's extremely poor insulation, would sap its strength without mercy. The man knew that in a short amount of time, the cold and unforgiving drafts blowing in from the small cracks high up in the walls would gradually overpower the deteriorating warmth radiating from the fireplace. This put the man in a very perilous situation. Freezing to death was not an uncommon manner of passing in the cold Alaskan wilderness. The man dwelled on it a moment and swiftly concluded he did not want to experience how it felt, though many had speculated it was a painless and peaceful way of expiring.

With great effort, he pushed himself off the bed and staggered to the water barrel for a drink. As he brought the dipper to his lips he remembered the sugar and dumped a liberal amount in. He swallowed the cold, sweet fluid hoping for a shot of energy and a shred of nourishment to temporarily stave off his immense hunger. He then retreated to the rocker and the inviting warmth of the fire. He removed his outer coverings and his hat, knowing it wouldn't be long before he'd have to put them back on.

"Well, what'll it be?" he thought as he gently rocked back and forth. "Am I gonna freeze to death first or die of hunger? Maybe the fever'll get me and I'll expire that way! Or maybe a grizzly will tunnel through the snow, break my door in, and eat me."

The man snickered a bit at his last thought, foolish as it was.

"That might not be all bad. He could stick me on a skewer and roast me like a marshmallow! What a sight that'd make. Interestin' way to go...without a shadow of a doubt."

The snicker strengthened into a full-fledged chuckle. The man had to laugh at himself and his precarious situation simply because there was little else he could do. He sat, rocked, looked out the window, waited, and rocked some more. Despite all his bodily pains and sickness, the man's primary vexation turned out to be sheer boredom and his inability to act. Being forced to do nothing aggravated him. He couldn't even get drunk, which irritated him above all else.

Fed up with sleeping, wanting to keep his mind occupied and not entirely focused on his intractable problems, the man stood up and looked around for something to read. He had no books, as reading for entertainment or knowledge had never interested him much. However, despite his reclusive nature, he did wonder what was happening in the world from time to time. Occasionally he would come across newspapers during his supply visits to Tanana. Some local merchant or businessman would always have one, usually discarded by a traveler, law enforcement official, politician, or just an enthusiastic adventurer passing through the region via California or Canada. The papers were always out of date by several days or sometimes weeks, but he always asked around town if any were available. He took what he could get and occasionally didn't mind parting with a few pennies to acquire one in good condition.

He searched all over the small cabin but found nothing. After angrily dwelling on it a bit, he remembered he had used his last few papers for kindling. He had read every word on every page before twisting them up and setting them alight beneath a bed of dry firewood. After returning to the rocker in disgust, the man used his limited imagination to visualize and reconstruct the paper's contents in his mind, specifically the articles he'd found most fascinating.

Recalling the most recent papers, he remembered being engrossed and alarmed at the reports of the resurgence of imperialism in Europe, which was causing many problems and pushing several countries toward political conflict. He wondered, like many, if Europe was on the path leading to war and what that meant for the United States. While in the Klondike, he had read accounts of U.S. involvement in the Spanish American War and how that helped solidify America as a growing world power. Would America's new position of strength influence the goings-on in Europe? He pondered the question and imagined how things might have changed since he'd read those accounts. For all he knew, Europe could be completely ablaze at that very moment. He couldn't know for sure. He was so very far away from it—and so much more.

Though thoughts of war and world politics intrigued him, his mind shifted toward a slightly older topic of news he found more captivating. He had read several issues of the *Los Angeles Times* reporting on the loss of a luxury passenger liner that had sunk in the North Atlantic. After reading the initial story, the man went out of his way to find as much printed information about the unfolding drama as he could. He was quite riveted by the conflicting reports about what had happened, particularly around the reported loss of life and the manner by which they died. Sensational accounts of icebergs, half-filled lifeboats, the freezing cold, panic-stricken passengers of all walks of life, and a ship deemed "unsinkable" reinvigorated the man's crippled imagination and made him think twice about life and those who live it—if only for a moment.

As the afternoon turned into evening, there was little sign of the storm letting up. The man coughed loudly, then listened to the remorseless wind pounding the walls of the cabin. The snow continued to drift and pile up against the window until it had risen halfway up the glass. Then the man heard the most unsettling sounds that struck unbridled fear into his heart. He looked upward, listening intently to the cracks and pops of the rafters as they began to buckle under the mounting weight of the built-up snow on the roof. The small pocket of warmth and shelter shielding the man from danger and keeping him alive was shrinking at an alarming rate. He began to wonder just how long his sturdy little cabin could hold back and keep out the unrelenting storm's fury.

The man now faced a danger that chilled his soul more than anything he had encountered since arriving in the wild many years earlier. His mind flashed back to the Chilkoot Trail and the constant, looming threat of avalanche. Being buried alive was a manner of death the man couldn't come to grips with. He had seen death in many forms back in the Klondike. Disease, malnutrition, exposure, accidents, outright murder—these were the kinds of casualties the man had grown immune to seeing. However, there was something uniquely disturbing and frightening about being encased under hundreds of pounds of rampaging snow. The thought of still being conscious, unable to move, slowly freezing and suffocating to death, was unbearable to him. It was a fate he wouldn't wish upon himself or his worst enemy—and it was a real, haunting threat now. The man silently concluded he'd rather fall asleep and just freeze to death rather than be caught in an avalanche.

The cabin grew darker and darker as the daylight hours ebbed away. The storm and rising snowfall increasingly blocked what little natural light penetrated the windows. The man was restless and on edge. He lurked from corner to corner in the dark like a miscreant waiting to commit a crime or a caged animal craving to be released from captivity. Soon the only light emanated from the pathetic little fire that had dwindled to nothing more than a tiny solitary flame atop a charred chunk of wood the size of the man's fist. Feeling the biting cold return in force, the man retrieved his furs and hat, hastily putting them back on. Knowing he might not survive the night with a dead fire, he made a rash decision and put all the remaining wood and kindling into the fireplace. The flames sparked back to life and soon a decent blaze was burning again.

The man cursed his luck and all the misfortunate circumstances that had brought him to his present state. His wood was now gone and he was forced to confront the thought of freezing to death, as his cabin would rapidly turn into an icebox soon after the fire died for good. The man returned to the rocking chair, covering his face with his aching hands. Fighting off the fatigue and rising delirium brought on by his now raging fever, his mind generated a thought that spurred him to action.

"I won't be beaten! To hell with the cold and to hell with this damn storm!" the man said with a renewed sense of survival that defiantly spat in the face of the dangers closing in on him.

Working only by aid of the dim firelight, the man grabbed his revolver that was lying on the floor and used the butt to hammer away at the protruding wooden pegs on the walls until they broke free. He collected the pieces and stacked them by the fireplace. Next he attacked the wooden table and chairs. Upending it, he snapped the table legs off using the power of his own legs. He then smashed away at the backs of both chairs, effectively reducing them to stools, and collecting the wooden debris, which he piled next to the fire. He then emptied his cabinets. After doing so he pounded and tore away at them, first ripping the doors off, then breaking free from the wall what was left. He put some of the wood directly onto the fire while the rest went into the newly created pile.

The man went to his trunk next. It was sturdily built, but could be broken apart and burned. He'd burn the clothes inside too if it came to that. All that remained was the rickety wooden bedframe. He pulled the thin mattress, blankets, and pillow off. He then stomped and smashed until it was nothing more than a pile of unrecognizable broken wood. He spared the rocker, mattress, pillow, and blankets. He wanted some semblance of comfort to remain should he be forcibly imprisoned by the storm a few more days and nights. The tabletop itself was wood, but it was too sturdy to break apart without heavier tools. The man left it alone for fear of injuring himself further or simply wearing himself out to the point of no recovery.

"There, I ain't gonna freeze to death tonight," he said smugly while sitting back down in the rocker.

The inside of the cabin was now in shambles. The man's meager supplies and what little gear he had were now scattered across the floor. The walls were bare and the furniture all but destroyed. The room looked as if a small tornado had torn through it. The mess made no impression whatsoever on the man. He sat rocking in front of the fire with his eyes closed, trying to stay focused on his next move. He'd feed the fire throughout the night and try to sleep when he could. In the morning he'd check the weather. If the storm broke, and the skies were clear, he'd smash through a window and tunnel his way out.

"I'll dig with my hands wrapped in cloth until I find my shovel, mittens, and my snowshoes. They should all be right by the door. I'll find 'em. Once I get my snowshoes on I'll start out for Tanana. Won't stop 'til I get there or drop dead tryin'. Maybe if it's clear enough I'll be able to clean off the roof before she caves in."

No sooner had he said that than a great crack thundered through the rafters, causing the man to jump out of the rocking chair. His chest pounded and he braced for what he thought for sure would happen next. He waited, but there was nothing. The roof held and the man wasn't crushed to death under a deluge of timber and snow. As the adrenaline wore off, he composed himself and kept close to the fire, feeding it the wooden refuse he had created. As time passed he occasionally drank more water sweetened with liberal amounts of sugar. His hunger grew more fierce, forcing him to try mixing flour with water and drinking it down. The white soupy mix tasted awful, leaving sugar as the only viable option for consumption. After several dippers of sugar and water, the man rose, unbuttoned his pants, and urinated into the washtub still full of bloody tepid water.

Soon it was time to try to sleep. The man felt more comfortable in the rocker than on the thin mattress. His throat was sore and filled with phlegm, causing him to choke and become dizzy when lying down. A sitting position was far more comfortable, he discovered. Occasionally he choked up the thick mucus and spat it out into the washtub. His head continued to burn with fever and his injured arm and shoulder pained him unmercifully. He had trouble thinking clearly and could feel the sickness rapidly overwhelming him. If he didn't get out soon, he'd succumb to his wounds before he even had a chance to make it to Tanana.

Unable to do anything about it now, he wedged his pillow between his head and the back of the rocker and tried to give his mind some much-needed rest, which in turn would hopefully help heal and revive his sick, battered body. He kept very close to the fire. So close that he started to feel uncomfortably warm. He reasoned that if the roof unexpectedly caved in, he'd be warned first by the sound of cracking lumber, which would give him a few seconds to dive into the hearth, curl up into a little ball, and avoid being crushed—a last-resort plan that could work, provided the fire had burned out. That was a risk he'd have to gamble on.

The hearth had an exceptionally wide and deep base. The man had it constructed this way to accommodate roasting large game on the spit. Even the brick chimney was wider than normal to facilitate a larger fire and a heavier volume of smoke. The man theorized that even if the wooden roof collapsed, the solid brick chimney would remain standing and keep him from being crushed to death. It might even prove to be a possible escape route. Those thoughts aside, for the time being the man simply needed the heat the hearth provided. He didn't want to think past that one essential function. After feeding the fire more scraps of wrecked furniture, he settled back in his rocker to try once again to sleep. Tomorrow, regardless of the severity of the weather, he would need to take some kind of action or else he was doomed. He no longer disputed or tried to ignore the point. He closed his sweat-drenched eyelids and tried to fall asleep. It wasn't long before his sick body shut down and the man's labored breathing intermixed with a heavy snore.

Over the course of the night he slept moderately well. Infrequently he woke at the sound of cracking timber above him, to feed the fire, or to clear his throat of mucus. He would painfully rise out of his rocker and step over to the washtub to spit and sometimes urinate. When finished he'd stumble back, sit down, and try to fall asleep again.

⁀) Chapter 7 (‿

One Last Chance

As the late nighttime gave way to the early-morning hours, the man woke to find himself in near total darkness. He groggily looked toward the fire and saw that it had nearly burned out. His hands and face were chilly and numb, forcing him to get up and grab more scraps of broken furniture to rekindle the blaze. Piling a good portion onto the hearth, he touched off a match and held the flickering flame to a piece of birch bark. Within minutes the fire came back to life. The flames danced upon the wood bringing much needed light and heat back into the cabin.

"Damn, you'd think I'd have one lousy candle," the man slurred in an aggravated, half-conscious tone, glancing toward his knocked-over lantern. "So damn dark...can't see nothin'."

He shivered by the fire until heat from the flames partially drove the chill from his body. Even in his weakened state, he remained awestruck by the insufferable cold. He had never experienced anything like it before and was reluctant to comprehend just how low the temperature had dropped.

"No thermometer on Earth could measure this confounded cold. God himself couldn't tolerate such miserable conditions," he muttered.

With resentment and spite, he aggressively threw more smashed furniture onto the blaze. As the light from the fire intensified, the man looked to the rear window for any signs of the storm letting up. A grim expression peppered with disbelief crept across his worn-out face. The snow was still falling and was over three-quarters of the way up the glass! At the rate it was accumulating, the man calculated it wouldn't be long before both windows were totally blocked, effectively barricading him in!

"God Almighty! How many ways of dying must a man face at once! I can handle one or two at a time...but four or five gangin' up on me? That's too much to ask of any man."

He looked skyward and defiantly declared, "I been tested before and I ain't broke yet. I'll beat this! God is my witness! I'll beat this and whatever evil force is behind it!"

Realizing that drastic measures were rapidly becoming his only option, the man thought about smashing the front window and digging out as soon as there was enough daylight to work by. He'd dig as hard and fast as his battered body would allow, climbing back into the cabin to thaw out by the fireplace when absolutely necessary. He'd need to stoke up the fire extra hot, gambling on prematurely exhausting his fuel before his work was complete. As soon as the window was shattered, the warm air would rapidly escape.

Waiting over an hour before taking any action, the man listened as the wind tapered off while watching the daylight slowly increase through the tiny bit of exposed glass.

"Storm's lettin' up. I can sense it. Maybe she'll break altogether and the skies'll clear," he said optimistically. "Then again, maybe this is just a moment of calm before she starts raging again. Either way, I got to do something now before it's too late!"

Injured, in pain, suffering from heavy fever and lack of adequate rest, he made the decision to act. In preparation for the blast of cold, he adjusted his hat and fur coverings so they fit securely to his body. He then bundled up his hands tight with shreds of old shirts taken from his trunk. What clothes remained went beside the fire to be burned when needed. Using the butt of the revolver and his legs, he then stomped and hammered at the wooden trunk until it resembled a pile of fractured kindling. It too went to the woodpile.

After stoking up the fire, he picked up the iron poker, and with a mighty thrust rammed it through the lower left pane of the front window. The glass shattered and exploded inward, bringing with it a small avalanche of snow. Caught off guard, the man was knocked off his feet by the sudden surge of unexpected force. As he hit the deck, his shoulder caught the edge of the nearby washtub. In an instant, the metal basin upended, spilling every drop of the vile blend of blood, water, and urine. The man looked on in horror as the large volume of reddish-brown liquid sloshed onto the hearth and flowed directly into the base of the fire. With a mighty sizzle, the flames were instantly drowned out!

"Goddammit," shouted the man, "What've I done?"

The room began to fill with white smoldering smoke as the man struggled to get to his feet. Water was everywhere. It covered most of the floor and saturated the hearth and everything around it. Even the man himself didn't make it through unscathed. Most of his backside was soaked. His furs, his shirt, his pants, moccasins, and socks were wet.

"My God," he exclaimed, realizing that one simple accident might have sealed his fate. He quickly stripped off his outer fur coverings and hat, tossing them near the mattress. He then unwrapped his hands from the now heavy and saturated rags. He quickly rubbed them together, blowing on them vigorously in an attempt to dry them as rapidly as possible.

Next he turned his full attention to the fireplace. He knew there wasn't a second to lose. He had always understood and appreciated the danger associated with extreme cold. He had lived with it for many years and was mindful of always being prepared to combat it. However, adding moisture brought the threat to a whole new level. To be wet in such extreme freezing conditions meant a person had only a short time to rectify things or else suffer rapid frostbite, then hypothermia, followed inevitably by death.

The man examined the hearth with conspicuous feelings of fear and dread that scampered up and down his spine. Water had completely soaked the burning wood and all the burnable scraps of clothing he had laid next to it. It settled into pools in and around the hearth, and everything the man had set aside to burn was now wet and unusable. To make matters worse, the snow that had cascaded in through the broken windowpane was now melting and refreezing into a solid icy mess. Cold air flowed in through the exposed windowpane. With the window broken, the man knew the cabin temperature would drop without mercy. He needed to act fast.

Quickly devising a plan, he went over to his mattress. The spilled water hadn't made it far enough across the floor to affect it.

"That's the answer," he said. "I'll tear open the mattress and use the dried straw and feathers to soak up the water in the fireplace. Then I'll break apart the rocker and build a new fire. I'll start with the pillow. That'd be easier."

He grabbed his pillow from the rocker and tore it open. He cleared away the sodden wood and set the pillow down in its place, hoping the exposed straw and feathers would soak up the excess water like a sponge.

"Yeah, that's it," the man said, seeing his idea begin to work. "Just a little bit more...then the mattress."

He cleared away the wet straw and feathers after they had soaked up as much water as they could. Grabbing the metal cooking spit, he punctured the mattress with the sharpened end and tore it open with his damp hands. Both were already feeling the numbing effects of the cold air flowing in like an icy river. Pulling out as much straw as he could, he stuffed it into the fireplace. After a few minutes he cleared it away, having successfully soaked up all the pools of water.

"Now the rocker."

With a mighty heave, the man picked up the rocking chair and slammed it down on a dry section of the floor. He cried out as his infected arm and shoulder throbbed with pain. The man looked at his injured limb, noticing his skin had turned a troubling color of dark red and purple underneath the bloody makeshift bandage. He knew he would lose it soon if not properly treated. Then he'd be viewed as a feeble old invalid... some Civil War veteran with exaggerated stories of battle to bore people with as soon as his black beard went gray. He cringed at the thought, wanting no such tag placed on him as his father had had.

He picked the rocker up again and smashed it down, this time with more ferocity and better results. The chair broke apart. He lined the base of the hearth with what remained of the dry mattress straw and placed the broken rocker fragments on top. The man looked on his hearth with renewed enthusiasm. Fire had saved his life many times before and it would now do so again. He was confident of that. Somehow it was inconceivable to him that such a simple accident could cause his ultimate demise.

"No matter now," he said to himself. "I'll be okay 'cause a man can take care of himself. I've proved it time and time again. I'll go on proving it, too. This won't be the death of me...I swear it!"

The stage had been set. Now it was time to bring out the main attraction. The man reached into his shirt pocket. His trembling hands were numb but still had feeling and use left in them. The sinking indoor temperature hadn't driven it from them yet. Feeling around for his tight bundle of matches, the man was surprised to find his pocket empty. He looked down and didn't see the familiar bulge in his shirt. Growing anxious, the man starting patting down his other pockets. Finding nothing, he began frantically searching all around. A horrifying thought crossed his mind as his wet moccasins splashed through the puddles on the floor. With a feeling of pure dread, he shifted his eyes downward. Carefully perusing the wet and debris-cluttered surface, he desperately hoped he'd find the priceless little bundle of sulfur-tipped sticks lying in a protected spot, undamaged, but most importantly—dry.

Then, in an instant, his eyes swept over a sight that caused his heart to sink and his stomach to churn with alarming distress. He reached down and batted away a metal cup resting on its side in a puddle of water. As the cup skidded away across the floor, the man saw what had lain partially hidden beneath it. Submerged in a shallow puddle of murky water rested the man's only chance for survival—the matches!

"Christ Almighty! How much does a fella need to suffer through to prove his worth?" cursed the man. "Apparently a fella's grit is measured by how he deals with soppin' wet matches in a cold drivin' Alaskan blizzard! Well I ain't gonna disappoint! I'll show you what a man can do!" He looked skyward as if he were calling out the Lord personally.

Unfortunately the man's resourcefulness didn't measure up to his angry boasting. Before the first idea popped into his mind, he clumsily dropped the match bundle back onto the wet floor. He cursed again loudly, then snatched it up before hurrying over to the fireplace. His hands shuddered as he tried to break off a single match. Once it was free, he struggled to maintain his grasp on the little fire-producing stick. Using both hands, he dragged the sulfur tip across the rough surface of the brick hearth. Nothing. He tried over and over again until the wet sulfur wore off completely. Frustrated and angry, the man cupped both quivering hands and brought the match bundle up close to his mouth. He blew hot breath onto it in hopes of quickly drying it out.

The man puffed heavily until he grew lightheaded. He peeled off another match. The sensation in his cold, wet hands was diminishing rapidly, making the match clutched in his fingers seem imperceptible unless he looked directly at it. He tried again to ignite the match only to witness the same discouraging results.

"Useless," he said after several unsuccessful attempts. He laid the match bundle down on the hearth, up high and in a dry spot. He tried to convince himself that all he had to do was wait a short time to allow the matches to dry; then he'd be able to strike one to life and build a new fire. However, the more he stared at the old, fragile, sodden bundle, the more he realized the futility of thinking fire could be derived from it. The matches were gone. They couldn't save him now.

The man lowered his head and let out a great sigh. His dejection heightened at the sight of ice crystals forming around the edges of the puddled water on his floor. He looked toward the broken window and felt the cold wind and snowflakes streaming inside. The icy air poured downward and spread across the room, blanketing everything in a frosty crystalline coating. As the cold air flowed, what was left of the cabin's warmth was rapidly escaping out the broken windowpane. Realizing he needed to act fast, the man grabbed the wet scraps of clothing he'd intended for the fire and stuffed them into the hole, doing his best to thoroughly plug the opening. Instantly the wet rags stiffened and froze hard. With the makeshift barrier in place, the river of cold air stopped. The man shivered and beat his arms hard against his chest and sides. After much effort, the blood resumed circulating again. Though very painful, the man welcomed the stinging in his hands and feet. He stomped around loudly, hoping the added movement would help warm him up more swiftly. He stopped only when he heard the unnerving sound of the roof timbers cracking again under the weight of the snow.

Taking a moment to calm down and gather his wits, the man sat down on a smashed chair—now resembling a stool—and wrapped his arms around his chest, burying his hands in his armpits. He curled up in a tight ball and shivered some warmth back into his body. He was lost. He closed his eyes, not knowing what to do. His mind drifted as foolish and unrealistic notions entered his thoughts. For a second he imagined picking up a telephone and calling for help or pecking out a distress message over a Marconi wireless telegraph. Both existed only in his imagination, of course. He'd never used a wireless but was familiar with telephones, having operated them years earlier in California. He yearned to hear a calming voice assuring him that help was on the way. He envisioned several large men breaking their way in, bringing food, warm clothes, medicine, and most importantly—fire.

"But who'd come?" the man said, opening his eyes and forcing his mind to embrace reality. In all his years in the Klondike and Alaska, he had never seen one telephone or even one telephone wire. He couldn't call for help and even if he could, who would help him? The man now began to question his resentful and reclusive lifestyle. He needed help badly and he needed it soon. As much as he hated interacting with others, he began to wish another human being would miraculously appear and deliver him from the harsh grip of certain death.

"How'd they get to me?" he thought. "Even if someone were crazy enough to be out in this shit, how'd they find me? No native would be dumb enough to venture out in this weather, and no white man from Tanana would dare risk this storm 'less he was drunk, crazy, stupid, or a combination of all three."

The man closed his eyes again and unexpectedly began to rethink the choices he had made in life. He wondered how things could have turned out differently if only he had stayed in California and not joined the gold rush. He wondered how much richer and happier he would have been if only he had remained in civilization and not chased fanciful dreams of gold and fortune in the wilds of the Yukon. When his thoughts turned to women he became alarmed and a great shudder went down his back. He opened his eyes and thrust his head upward.

"What the hell's wrong with me?" he asked, the bitterness return-ing to his voice. "I've never needed nothin' or nobody to get me out of a jam. I still ain't dead yet," he added with arrogant determination as he pushed himself up off the stool.

The man was not accustomed to feelings of compassion, tender-ness, neediness, or regret, as he considered them useless and weak emo-tions. His years in the wild had hardened him and driven away almost every form of gentleness his soul had ever possessed. To show selfless-ness or any level of sympathy or care toward anything or anyone but himself was to invite betrayal or death, and the man wanted nothing to do with that. Fighting the urge to surrender to his suppressed softer na-ture, and to his predicament, the man tried to clear his feverish mind and devise a new plan to save himself.

"If only I had means to build a fire and beat back this brutal cold!" he sputtered as he began to pace in order to keep his blood flowing. The puddles of water had already turned to ice beneath his feet. He blew on his hands to dry them and keep them somewhat warm. He knew it wouldn't be much longer before his damp clothes would freeze, becom-ing a conductor to the cold rather than a protector from it.

The man hurried over to his mattress and wrapped his blanket around his shoulders. He then got an idea. The blanket was dry and therefore still useful. He used his cooking spit to puncture the center of the blanket, ripping a hole large enough to poke his head through. He then found a piece of rope and tied it around his waist to keep the blanket snug against his body. Examining his fur hat, he concluded that it was only partially wet on the outside. The inside was still dry; therefore it was safe to wear. He put it on.

Coughing loudly, the man spit up some blood. He struggled to keep his head clear, although the pain in his injured arm was becoming unbearable. He knew he wouldn't last another night. Even if he could fend off the cold he was sure he'd succumb to his injuries or the fever af-ter falling unconscious—that's if the roof didn't cave in and kill him out-right first. He looked again to the door, knowing it could not be opened. He looked at the rear window and saw that the drifting snow had nearly blocked it completely. He looked to the damaged front window and saw that it too was obstructed beyond any hope for escape. A new problem revealed itself when the man realized that he had very little natural light. There was nothing to produce light in the cabin, and the snow-blocked windows kept out most of what little daylight there was. There was just enough light to see, but the man knew it wouldn't last long. He looked out the tiny slit of unobstructed rear window and listened hard to the sounds of the weather outside.

"She's still quiet...for now," the man said, but then he added, "Skies could go black at any time and leave me in the darkness, entombed here under a hunnert pounds of snow! Hell if I let that happen!"

The man feared breaking the front window any further and trying to tunnel out. The risk of more snow plunging uncontrollably inward was too great. He couldn't stomach the thought of being buried alive by an avalanche of snow. The rear window promised the same potential for disaster so the man ignored it. He also feared how quickly his failing hands would freeze and become useless the second they got wet again. Even if he could sufficiently wrap them in shreds of his dry blanket, he still feared they wouldn't last long enough to make it out. Instead, he thought of something else. He tore strips from his blanket to wrap around his hands, but not to use as protection while digging, only to keep them as warm and dry as possible. He had other plans in mind.

Just then a massive snap sounded from above. The man jerked around and looked up. To his horror, the roof's main support beam had a huge crack running the length of it. The roof now sagged noticeably—it was buckling under the heavy weight of the built-up snow.

In desperation, the man went to the fireplace and furiously cleared away all the kindling and debris. He scrunched down, then pulled himself up inside the chimney. The man was tall and lean and was happily surprised at how easily he fit up the simple brick smokestack. It was not very tall, the man thought. Fifteen, seventeen, maybe twenty feet? Was it possible to climb up and out? Just maybe. But how?

The man squeezed out and started looking around the room for anything he thought might help him. He bundled up his sugar, salt, some wood scraps, the wet matches, a metal cup, and whatever else he deemed useful in his outer fur coverings, tying it with rope. Before doing so, he spread some salt onto the wet garments, hoping it would help dry them. He tied the loose end around his waist. Next he grabbed the two stools and set them close to the hearth. He picked up his revolver and tucked it into his belt, then placed the cooking spit by the stools. Lastly he retrieved the iron poker, keeping it handy for the idea he had brewing in his mind.

Another sharp crack thundered from above as the roof's main support beam buckled further. The man, ignoring all the pain, sickness, and numbness wrapped up in his freezing body, worked fanatically, knowing that there wasn't much time. He stacked one of the stools on top of the other and positioned them as far back into the hearth as he could. Scrunching down again, he wiggled his way in and carefully stood up. He stepped up onto the stools, bracing himself against the chimney walls in case the chairs collapsed under his unsteady weight. To his delight, the stools held and he was ready to initiate the next part of his plan.

"Now, with just a little luck…God willing."

The man stepped down and reached for the cooking spit. He climbed back up on the stools and raised the metal rod above his head. Feeling around in the faint light creeping down the chimney, he searched for an indentation or hole in the brick mortar. He was glad to find many spots where the mortar had crumbled away, forming gaps between the bricks large enough to fit his fingers or the tips of his moccasins. Upon finding a suitable spot, he placed the sharp pointed end of the spit at an angle and drew his revolver. With the butt end of the gun, he pounded away at the metal rod, driving it firmly into the brick and mortar.

"Son-of-a-bitch may hold," muttered the man as he tried to work the rod up and down, testing its strength. It didn't budge and felt hard and secure. The man was confident it could support a good deal of weight—specifically, *his* weight. "Now comes the real test," he thought.

The man climbed out and retrieved more rope and the iron poker. With the poker in hand, he tied the rope securely around and through the looped handle. He then tied the other end around his waist and positioned the stools directly under the rod. He climbed back up on the stools, then reached up and grabbed the metal rod with both hands. He pulled himself up using his legs and feet as support wherever he could find a toehold in the deteriorating brick mortar. With much struggle and excruciating pain coursing through his injured arm, he managed to pull and squirm himself up enough to get his legs over the bar, allowing him to sit on it. Then, finding two good handholds above, he pulled himself up until he stood erect on the metal rod.

He breathed heavily and his weakened legs shuddered. His fingers were cut open and blood trickled down from the exposed tips. He was lightheaded, dizzy, and twice felt like vomiting. Not knowing how long the rod would support his weight, he gingerly pulled up the rope attached to the iron poker. Looking upward, he estimated he had between seven and nine feet left to reach the top of the chimney. He raised the poker, which had a hooked end, hoping to snag the top edge of the chimney and pull himself out. Unfortunately, he was a few feet short and couldn't reach the top.

"Damn," he shouted, coughing up phlegm mixed with blood.

He extended the poker as far as his arm would reach, but it wasn't good enough. Standing in the dark, now covered in filthy black soot, his cold, tired, battered body at the breaking point, he had one final idea. He tossed the poker upward, hoping the curved end would catch the top edge of the chimney like a grappling hook. The first attempt failed as the poker clanked against the side and dropped to the floor. Frustrated, the man pulled the rope until the poker was back in his hands. He tried again—with the same result. He repeated the process several more times without success.

"God, help me outta this devilish trap!" he shouted as he desperately banged the poker against the chimney. The futile act accomplished nothing except to rain dislodged soot down upon him. He coughed and found it harder and harder to breathe. His mind became increasingly unclear and his strength was waning beyond recovery. Unable to focus, the man became incapable of thinking past the immediate problem. All he could ponder was how to get up and out of the chimney. No other thought or feeling entered his head.

Then, as if a massive bolt of lightning had clapped down from the heavens, the roof's support beam gave out with an unmerciful thunderous crack! The man closed his eyes, expecting to be killed at any second.

Instead, the roof slowly started to cave in at the very center. He heard the rafters buckle and snap one by one under the immense pressure until the whole structure folded on both sides. A second later there was another loud sound: that of crunching brick as the base of the chimney crumpled inward. The man extended his arms to brace himself as the entire chimney began to topple. Soot and loose mortar broke free, striking the man from above, but he held on—until the battered chimney came to rest at an obtuse 130-degree angle.

"Jesus...Lord in heaven. Have I been saved?" the man uttered in a raspy, almost incoherent voice.

As it fell inward, the chimney had landed mostly intact on a large mound of snow at an angle at which the man could crawl up and escape. He mustered what little remaining strength he had and excruciatingly inched his way up on his knees and elbows. The cold wind and snow blew into the chimney with renewed ferocity—the storm had resumed its onslaught. Just as the man was within reach of the top, he raised the poker and jabbed at the flimsy wooden cap designed for keeping snow, rain, or pesky animals from entering the chimney. The cap was badly damaged and easy to poke away. Once it was clear, he reached up, placing his hands on the edge. Instantly they numbed once exposed to the frigid air of the storm. With one final effort the man tried to pull himself out, only to be stopped like a dog on a taut leash. The man looked down and saw the rope tied around his waist.

"The bundle!"

The base of the chimney was caved in. The rope he had attached to the bundle of supplies wrapped in his outer fur coverings was now pinned under a heavy pile of rubble. Without delay, the man slid down to gain some slack and tried to untie the rope from his waist. Shocked, he discovered it was no use. His hands had gone completely dead! There was no feeling in his fingers. His feet were only marginally better, but he could tell they would leave him also, in just a matter of minutes. He was forced to accept that the cold had finally driven all life from his extremities—forever.

"You think this is the end don't you?" he said, not knowing if he should be addressing God or the Devil. "This ain't the end," he stated defiantly, adding, "I'll show you what a man can do...even with two dead hands!"

He felt a jagged piece of mortar sticking into his back. He positioned himself the best he could, making the rope tight. He began rubbing his waist into the sharp fragment still partially yet firmly embedded into the brick. He heard his blanket tear then the clothes beneath. He felt the mortar dig into his skin and the blood flow down his leg until it reached his foot where now he could feel nothing. Still he rubbed harder knowing the rope was fraying with each strained, painful motion. Then, miraculously the rope broke and limply fell away into the darkness below.

"That's what a man does...that's what a *man* can do," he said as his injured arm cramped, locking up tight, becoming useless. "No matter...I still ain't gonna die in here."

He crawled up, reaching the top. With one last thrust, his beleaguered legs pushed him out of the chimney onto the snow. He sank in nearly waist deep. The man's black and bloody appearance contrasted sharply with the snowy white surroundings that dominated as far as the eye could see. The man opened his eyes wide as the snow and wind pelted his face. He looked in all directions but couldn't recognize one landmark. Not one earthly feature looked familiar to him. Everything was just a sea of white. He looked toward where he knew the mountains and the lake should be but saw nothing—nothing but driving snow that swallowed up everything. No forest, no lake, no mountains, no life anywhere—just an endless expanse—a desert of snow.

It all seemed surreal. The man wondered if he was still alive or dead. Was this featureless landscape covered in endless layered blankets of windswept snow his personal version of hell? He couldn't be sure. His failing mind wasn't sure of anything anymore. As all the feeling went out of his arms and legs and the sting slowly ebbed away from his frostbitten cheeks, the man felt very sleepy and his eyelids became heavy. With one last desperate gesture, he forced himself to look in the direction he thought led to Tanana. He willed his arms and legs to move, but there was no hope left. The man dipped his head and spat up some blood. His labored breathing began to slow and settle into short ineffectual gasps.

His throat was swollen and his severely chapped lips could barely move, as they were encased in frozen blood. Still, the man felt it necessary to speak his last words.

"Well...guess freezing to death wins," he uttered, recalling the numerous ways he'd thought he might die. "Hope it's quick and painless, like I heard many old-timers tell. Maybe it won't be so bad. Maybe I'll just go to sleep and wake up dead...if I ain't already dead, that is. Goddamn, how'd it come to this? This world just ain't no damn good. Never had a bit of use for any of it," he cursed with simmering insolence.

One final surge of panic struck him as he realized death was drawing near. He fought to stay conscious but it was no use. His head dipped and his eyes closed for what he thought would be the final time. A moment passed and something compelled the man to look up. With great effort, he raised his head skyward. He opened his eyes wide as his jaw dropped open.

"I...I...I must be dreamin', or else I surely am dead," said the bewildered man. His glassy eyes looked toward the angry sky and saw a vision—an image, a lovely image surrounded by a heavenly glow of light. He became fixated on it as if nothing else in the world existed.

He saw the face of a tender young woman of twenty-three looking down upon him. Her eyes were emerald green and her skin smooth and pale. Her plump lips were bright red and her strawberry blond hair was long with thick, flowing curls. Beautiful as she was, her face appeared troubled and a deep sadness was evident. The man knew this woman— he knew her well.

"Eveline!" was all he said. Suddenly the man saw other visions. He saw himself young and clean-shaven, dressed in a suit and hat walking the streets of San Francisco. He saw a smile sweep over his face as Eveline came and took his arm. The two happily strolled along until the vision faded. The man looked farther, seeing images of his mother and father back in Massachusetts. He saw a kindness and a nurturing quality in his mother's face he swore he had never noticed in his youth. He saw patience and virtue in the face of his father, whose body was maimed by the madness of war. The two appeared together, happily hand in hand, before slowly fading away.

The man next saw visions of a boy running carefree through a field. He laughed and jumped and ran and spun in every direction before stopping to climb an old oak tree. He rested lazily on a limb without a care in the world. The man recognized the boy as well—it was he. The sky went dark again. The man lowered his head. Though his body had shut down almost entirely, his heart still beat. It filled with grief and anguish as well as tenderness, forgiveness, benevolence, and also regret. For a moment, all the mistrust, anger, and bitterness, so characteristic of the man for so long, had been driven from it fully.

"I'm sorry...I'm so sorry. I'm Harrison T. Dawes, only son of Geoffrey and Madelyn Dawes of Springfield, Massachusetts, and I had my whole life in front of me. I let my darker side govern my actions. Where did it get me? What've I accomplished in life that's noble or worthy of a man? Nothin', not a goddamn thing! I shunned those who tried to help me and let true love slip through my greed-infested fingers. I never fathered a child and gave it a chance to have a loving family. I let my petty shortcomings and avarice isolate me from all those who mattered most! I was blind, dishonest, disrespectful...most of all ignorant...ignorant to the true joys of life! God help me, God save me. God forgive me for the time I've wasted."

Harrison looked up one last time and again saw a vision of his lost love Eveline. This time her face showed an expression of understanding and compassion that struck his heart warmly. The last thing he saw was his dear, sweet Eveline smiling mischievously as she had done many times before, a lifetime ago. Her image faded, and with it went the life of Harrison T. Dawes—forever.

About the Author

CHRISTOPHER MORIN was born, raised, and currently resides in Portland, Maine. He received a B.A. in Journalism from the University of Maine at Orono. He is a history enthusiast and has enjoyed creative writing since penning his first short story back in second grade.